Become a sta... Wit...

This three-level reading series is designed for pre-readers, beginning readers or improving readers and is based on popular Ranger Rob episodes. The books feature common sight words used with limited grammar. Each book also offers a set number of target words. These words are noted in bold print and are presented in a picture dictionary in order to reinforce meaning and expand reading vocabulary.

BUDDING RANGER

For pre-readers to read along

- 125-175 words
- Simple sentences
- Simple vocabulary and common sight words
- Picture dictionary teaching 6 target words

APPRENTICE RANGER

For beginning readers to read with support

- 175-250 words
- Longer sentences
- Limited vocabulary and more sight words
- Picture dictionary teaching 8 target words

SUPER RANGER

For improving readers to read on their own or with support

- 250-350 words
- Longer sentences and more complex grammar
- Varied vocabulary and less-common sight words
- Picture dictionary teaching 10 target words

CrackBoom! Books is an imprint of Chouette Publishing (1987) Inc.

Adaptation of the animated series: Anne Paradis
All rights reserved.
Illustrations: Nelvana Ltd

 Ranger Rob is a trademark of Nelvana Limited.

Chouette Publishing would like to thank the Government of Canada
and SODEC for their financial support.

Bibliothèque et Archives nationales du Québec
and Library and Archives Canada cataloguing in publication

Paradis, Anne, 1972-
[Amour de caméléon. English]

My pet ranger/adaptation, Anne Paradis; illustrations, Nelvana ltd;
translation, David Warriner.

(Read with Ranger Rob. Level 2: apprentice ranger)
Translation of: Un amour de caméléon.
Target audience: For children aged 3 and up.

ISBN 978-2-89802-007-0 (softcover)

I. Warriner, David, translator. II. Nelvana (Firm), illustrator. III. Title.
IV. Title : Amour de caméléon. English.

PS8631.A713A6313 2019   jC843'.6   C2018-942474-5
PS9631.A713A6313 2019

Printed in China
10 9 8 7 6 5 4 3 2 1   CHO2046 NOV2018

READ WITH
RANGER ROB

Level 2
APPRENTICE RANGER

My Pet Ranger

Adaptation of the animated series: Anne Paradis
Illustrations: Nelvana Limited

CRACKBOOM!

Leon is a baby **chameleon**.

Rob takes Leon into
the jungle.

Dakota greets Leon.

She is planning a **show** about **chameleons**.

Stomper sees a **blue chameleon**.

Rob sees a **red chameleon.**

Chameleons can change color.

Rob takes Leon on a tour.

Leon climbs the **trees** of the jungle with Rob.

Then, Leon visits the forest.
There are lots of
trees in the forest.

Leon visits the desert, too.

It is very **hot** in the desert.

Brrr! It is **cold** in
the Frosty Fields.

Leon prefers when it is **hot**.

Leon returns to the jungle.

Leon is not **cold**
anymore.

Suddenly, Leon
changes color.

He turns **red** and **green**.

Rob's clothes are **red** and **green** too.

Stomper is **blue** and white.

Leon joins the other **chameleons**.

Leon is **green** again.

Everything is ready
for the **show**.
The visitors arrive.

Welcome to the **chameleon show**!

Picture Dictionary

tree/trees

show

hot

cold

red

green

blue

chameleon